Cat Likes Red

CHRISTOPHER RUSSO

HOLIDAY HOUSE • NEW YORK

Cat likes **red**.

Red is nice.

Cat likes **yellow**.

Yellow is nice.

Cat likes **green**.

Green is nice.

Cat likes **blue**.

Blue is nice.

Cat likes **pink**.

Pink is nice.

Cat likes **orange**.

Orange is nice.

Cat likes **black**.

Black is nice.